Out of Sterno

by Deborah Zoe Laufer

A SAMUEL FRENCH ACTING EDITION

SAMUEL
FRENCH
FOUNDED 1830

NEW YORK HOLLYWOOD LONDON TORONTO

SAMUELFRENCH.COM

IMPORTANT BILLING AND CREDIT REQUIREMENTS

All producers of *OUT OF STERNO must* give credit to the Author of the Play in all programs distributed in connection with performances of the Play, and in all instances in which the title of the Play appears for the purposes of advertising, publicizing or otherwise exploiting the Play and/or a production. The name of the Author *must* appear on a separate line on which no other name appears, immediately following the title and *must* appear in size of type not less than fifty percent of the size of the title type.

In addition the following credit *must* be given in all programs and publicity information distributed in association with this piece:

Professional Premiere Production:
PORTLAND STAGE COMPANY, Portland, Maine
Anita Stewart, Executive & Artistic Director
Camilla Barrantes, Managing Director

Originally developed by CHERRY LANE THEATRE,
Angela Fiordellisi, Artistic Director

OUT OF STERNO received its world premiere production at the Portland Stage Company (Anita Stewart, Executive & Artistic Director; Camilla Barrantes, Managing Director) in Portland, Maine on March 6, 2009. It was directed by Casey Stangl; the set design was by Anita Stewart; the costume design was by Chris Rumery; the lighting design was by Bryon Winn; the sound design was by Stephen Swift; and the production stage manager was Myles C. Hatch. The Cast was as follows:

DOTTY	Janice O'Rourke
ZENA	Patricia Buckley
DAN	Phillip Taratula
HAMEL	Torsten Hillhouse

CHARACTERS

DOTTY - 23. Childlike and loving and hopeful, bursting with intense enthusiasm for everything. She refuses to think ill of anyone.

HAMEL - 30s-40s. Dotty's thuggish husband. Very very very not smart. Loves his wife needs her for everything, but is prey to other urges. Much more stupefied than angry or threatening.

ZENA - 30s-40s The proprietress of Zena's Beauty Emporium. Miss Triboro Area for two years running. Tough as nails.

DAN - Magically transforms himself into every other character in the play, including:

DELIVERY MAN

TAXI DRIVER

WAITER

MRS. CUTHBERT

MRS. PEABODY

BARB

SALLIE MAE

MAN ON THE BUS

PLACE

The play takes place in various locations in Sterno, a small town somewhere in America.

TIME

The time is now.

Each location can be defined by one or two key elements which should wheel in or fly out as if by magic – the kitchen table, the Emporium sign, the cosmetics table. At the opening, the tone of the play is very bright and presentational. *PeeWee's Playhouse* meets *A Doll's House* meets *Alice in Wonderland.* As Dotty ventures further from her confines, the tone get darker and more realistic.

To my parents, who told me all the right things.

With special thanks to Marsha Norman, Chris Durang and The Cherry Lane Alternative.

ACT I

(**DOTTY**'s kitchen table. It's a mess. Paints and clay and odd papier-mache sculptures are mixed in with pots and pans and food remains.

Crude but vibrant paintings and collages cover the walls. They are pictures of items we see in the kitchen itself – the table, a chair, the refrigerator.

There is a television set with a VCR facing the audience far downstage.

A clock tower chimes six times.

We hear **DOTTY** from offstage.)

DOTTY. Holy Moly!

(She rushes in covered from head to toe in paint and clay and sparkles. Her hair is up but spilling down.

She carries a big lump of chopped meat. Clears a space at the table with her elbows, wipes her hands on her house dress, and begins to make patties.)

(to the audience)

Six o'clock! And I haven't even started Hamel's dinner!

(She forms a lovely circular patty, then with her finger punches out two eyes, a nose, and a mouth and holds it up to show the audience.)

Like my Mama always said, "Doesn't cost any extra to make things beautiful!"

(She places the patty gingerly in a frying pan.)

Hamel's a dreamboat.

(She pulls a photo out of her pocket.)

This is him.

7

(She kisses the photo, then brings it down to the audience and hands it to someone in the first row.)

You can pass that around. He'll be here soon, so don't worry if it doesn't get to you in the back.

(Back to her patty-making.)

First time I laid eyes on Hamel, I passed right out. He's got that kind of charisma. I was sixteen. He moved to our town from someplace else. No one had ever done that before so there was a lot of commotion. Every time I heard about him, I could feel my ears get hot.

Then June 3rd, 2:30 p.m., I was at Joyner's store getting myself a chocolate Yoohoo and in walks Hamel. He looks me over, does this *(click click)* with the side of his teeth and says, "Hey, kid."

Well. When I came to, I see Hamel standing over me. He goes –

(She whistles.)

"What a nut!"

And my life has never been the same since!

Here. I have a reenactment.

(She goes to the TV, turns it on, presses "play" on the VCR. As it is starting:)

This TV doesn't get channels, so I watch this a lot. The actors don't really capture the magic, but this is basically the way it happened.

*(The picture comes up and we see the scene played out with community theater-type actors. When it is done, **DOTTY** turns it off and rewinds the tape.)*

And a week later we were married!

Now we live in Sterno, which is a huge huge city, and Hamel works at the Mobil oil station, and we're so much in love! It's like a fairytale, it really is.

I don't exactly know anyone here, yet. Hamel doesn't much like for me to talk with other people. He's so crazy about me he wants me all to himself! I love that.

I bet it took a while for my mama to get used to never seeing or talking to me but like she always said, "Make your man the center of your world and you'll never get lost."

I haven't actually ever even left this apartment! Not since we moved in seven years ago.

(Reacting to the audience.)

No, no – that's a-ok with me. This is just about the greatest place on earth! All this and at six fifteen sharp, Hamel himself.

(Looks at a kitchen clock.)

Four minutes to Hamel time! So any of you ladies who are prone to fainting, get out your smelling salts!

*(The phone rings. **DOTTY**, perplexed, no longer recognizes the sound. It rings again. She hastily searches through the rubble for it.)*

Goodness, who could that be?

*(She answers the phone. We can hear **ZENA**'s conversation as well. **ZENA** has a thick husky Bronx accent. She sounds like she could snap your neck with a look.)*

Hello?

ZENA. Gimme Hamel.

DOTTY. Oh, he should be here in three more minutes. Would you care to leave a message?

(She stands poised with a pen.)

ZENA. You tell him, get your ass to Jimmy's by six-thirty sharp. Zena waits for nobody.

DOTTY. *(taking it down)* Get your a...

(Her pen doesn't work. Looking around madly)

Oh fiddlesticks! My pen just gave out. Goodness, I've got paints and such everywhere, but when I want to find a pen...

ZENA. Six thirty sharp or he can go fuck himself.

(She hangs up.)

DOTTY. Hello? Hello? Hmmm. Well, that certainly sounded important! Can you remember what she said her name was? Zenith? Such an exotic name! Hamel meets the most interesting people.

(The doorbell rings. Again, **DOTTY** *is stymied. It rings again.)*

What an exciting day I'm having. Excuse me, won't you?

(She goes to the door. **DAN** *is there as a delivery guy.)*

DAN. Delivery for Mr. Hamel Burr.

DOTTY. Goodness! That's my husband.

(proudly, with a wink to the audience)

I'm Dotty. His wife.

DAN. Here you are, Ma'am.

(hands her a long box)

We're not supposed to snoop, but it sure smells like flowers!

DOTTY. Flowers! My!

DAN. Sign right here, Ma'am.

DOTTY. Why certainly.

(to the audience)

Ummm…do you have a pen?

DAN. Sure do, Ma'am. Comes with the job.

DOTTY. Thanks!

(She signs and takes the package.)

DAN. Bye, Ma'am. Someone sure must love you!

(He leaves.)

*(***DOTTY** *opens the box. It's a dozen long-stemmed roses.)*

DOTTY. Oh my goodness good gracious me! Didn't I tell you? I'm the luckiest girl in the whole United States of America!

(We hear footsteps down the hall.)

Do you hear footsteps??? I hear footsteps!!! He's coming! It's Hamel! He'll be here any second!

(**HAMEL** *enters hurriedly. He is removing a greasy ser-vice station uniform as he enters. As he passes through the room and out to the bedroom!*)

HAMEL. Hey, Kid. *(click click)*

(*He exits.*)

DOTTY. That was him!!! That was Hamel!!! Isn't he a dream-boat? Did you get a whiff of motor oil as he passed through? Makes me dizzy!

HAMEL. Hey, Kid! Dotty! Where's my magenta shirt? The shiny one.

DOTTY. Do you hear the way he talks? Magenta. Just being in his presence I'm soaking up so much culture and nuance.

HAMEL. Where the fuck is it?

DOTTY. Did you try the closet, Dear?

HAMEL. Hey, where's my Old Spice?

DOTTY. He's going to wear his men's perfume! Wait till you smell him. Oh boy. It's on the dresser, Dear.

HAMEL. Huh.

DOTTY. Goodness! I almost forgot! You got a telephone call!

HAMEL. Huh?

DOTTY. A Zenith I believe she said. Sounded very impor-tant.

HAMEL. Oh, shit. What she say?

DOTTY. Well, my pen ran out so I didn't get it all down, but I think it had something to do with the time, and with you making sure that…

(**HAMEL** *comes racing out. He is wearing his magenta shirt, very tight leather pants, cowboy boots and his hair slicked back.*)

HAMEL. Gotta go. Bye kid.

DOTTY. Go?

HAMEL. *(He tosses his uniform at* **DOTTY** *as he passes.)* Wash this, will ya?

DOTTY. Why certainly. Hamel! You look so…

HAMEL. Yeah. I got a…an important…business meetin'.

DOTTY. A business meeting? At this hour?

HAMEL. …dinner. A business…meal! See ya kid.

DOTTY. But, Hamel.

HAMEL. Don't leave the apartment!

DOTTY. Hamel…

HAMEL. Like my Papa always said, "*Don't leave the apartment.*" (*click click*) Bye, Kid.

DOTTY. Hamel, these flowers came and I…

HAMEL. Oh, shit! Right! The flowers.

> (*He grabs them on his way out.*)

> Thanks, Kid. See ya later. Don't wait up.

> *Don't leave the apartment.*

> (*He exits.*)

DOTTY. A business meal. My goodness. Sounds very important.

> (*She thinks about this. Works just a bit harder to be positive.*)

> Hamel is so career minded and motivated! He's probably off meeting someone very prominent in the… service station industry. My Hamel won't be pumping gas forever! You mark my…

> (*As she frets anxiously with the uniform a picture falls out of the pocket.*)

> Heavens!

> (*She picks it up and stares at it.*)

> A girly picture. A nude girly picture in Hamel's pocket! How in the world could that have…

> (*She thinks about it a moment, recovers nicely.*)

> Those guys at the filling station! Such kidders! I bet Hamel didn't even know this was in there. We'll have a good chuckle over this when he gets home, I don't mind telling you!

> (*She has a good chuckle. Then happens to turn it over and read the back.*)

Zena's Beauty Emporium. Wasn't that the name of the young lady who called here earlier? What an odd coincidence…

(brightly) Guess I better get to the wash! Down in the basement they have three machines, can you imagine?

(The doorbell rings.)

Now, who could that be?

Who is it?

DAN. Taxi.

DOTTY. Taxi?

(She shrugs to the audience, opens the door and it is **DAN**, *now dressed as a* **TAXI DRIVER**. *Different voice, maybe Slavic. Maybe a moustache.)*

DAN. Here am I to pick up Mr. Hamel Burr. For destination being Jimmy's Hideaway.

DOTTY. *(to audience)* Wasn't that the name of the place Zenith mentioned?

(to **DAN***)* Hamel already left. But he was going to a business meal.

DAN. Ah, yes. I see this so often in my line of work.

DOTTY. What?

DAN. The man, the husband, he says he is going to business meal. Did he bring with him the red roses?

DOTTY. Yes, he did!

DAN. Did he wear tight pants and magenta shirt?

DOTTY. Why yes! That's amazing.

DAN. Cowboy boots.

DOTTY. Right!

DAN. Ah. This is too bad. Oh well, you are young. No babies yet, yes?

DOTTY. Yes. I mean, no. Of course, I'm hoping.

(to audience)

I love children, don't you?

DAN. Well. It is good you wait. The next husband, no?

DOTTY. The next...

DAN. So we go, yes?

DOTTY. No! I'm really sorry for your trouble. I would pay you, but I don't have any money...

(A twenty dollar bill floats to the floor.)

Golly!

DAN. *(taking the twenty)* Thank you very much. So we go see husband. What he is doing, no?

DOTTY. I don't want to see. I mean, there's nothing to see.

DAN. Then you go see nothing. We have good laugh.

DOTTY. I don't want to laugh. I want to stay here. It's a little slice of heaven on earth and I want to stay here forever and ever. I think you should go away now.

(to audience)

I think he should go away.

DAN. Maybe you are right. Maybe it is just meal. After all, it is not like you find nude girly picture in pocket, right?

DOTTY. Oh dear.

DAN. You have maybe big hat? Trench coat? Sunglasses?

DOTTY. I'm not supposed to leave the apartment. I've never...

DAN. You change. I wait.

*(**DOTTY** thinks for a moment. Looks to the audience. LIGHT SHIFT.*

Tango music. Lights up on a table at Jimmy's Hideaway. The lights are seductive. There is smoke in the air.

***HAMEL** and **ZENA** are having a heated argument which we can see but not hear. **ZENA** wears a hat, trench coat and sunglasses. She looks sexy and mysterious.*

***DOTTY** enters in a hat, trench coat and sunglasses. They are far too big and she looks like a mushroom.*

***DAN**, now as a waiter with attitude, approaches her.)*

DAN. Table?

DOTTY. No. Thank you. I'm just looking.

DAN. There's no just looking.

(A chair appears out of the darkness and **DOTTY** *plops into it.)*

I'll give you a moment to decide.

(He disappears. The tango music swells. **ZENA** *and* **HAMEL***'s fight becomes more ferocious. They rise from their chairs, gesturing madly at each other.)*

DOTTY. *(to audience)* This is a very intense business meal! Hamel is so passionate about his work! Well, I guess I can go now.

(As she rises to go, **ZENA** *slaps* **HAMEL** *across the face hard, three times.)*

Heavens!

*(***ZENA** *is about to stalk off when, tango style,* **HAMEL** *grabs her hand, twirls her around several times and throws her back into a deep dip. He holds her there for a long moment. She slaps him one more time, and then they passionately kiss.)*

Oh dear.

(A wave of nausea hits her.)

I think I'm going to be sick!

(LIGHT SHIFT)

*(***DOTTY***'s apartment, the next evening.)*

DOTTY. I'm so confused about last night. Was that really Hamel? It was so dark. And what was the name of the lady who called? It's all jumbled in my head now. The one thing I feel certain of is that there's an excellent explanation for all of this, and all my Hamel needs is the opportunity to explain. Like my Mama always said, "There's nothing so horrible it can't be explained away!" I'll be tough, but fair. I'll say...

(Dream music plays. **HAMEL** *enters in his uniform.)*

Hamel, are you aware that you never came home last night?

HAMEL. I didn't?

DOTTY. Are you aware that there are nude girly pictures in your uniform pocket?

HAMEL. Those guys at the station!

DOTTY. Are you aware that your business meal at Jimmy's took on a very unbusinesslike tone?

HAMEL. Dotty, Honey. Let me explain.

DOTTY. Yes?

HAMEL. It was just someone who looked like me!

DOTTY. Really?

HAMEL. We were just rehearsing a play!

DOTTY. Really?

HAMEL. It was the lighting, you were hallucinating, it was a dream, it was my evil twin, you didn't really see what you thought you were seeing at all!

DOTTY. *(to the audience)* I knew there had to be a good explanation.

HAMEL. May I kiss you, my darling?

DOTTY. Put on the magenta shirt and then I will be kissed.

(He runs off.

HAMEL *enters from the other side.)*

HAMEL. Hey, Kid. *(click, click)*

(He walks through, hardly giving her a nod.)

DOTTY. Hamel…Where have you…

HAMEL. *(from offstage)* Got a business meal.

DOTTY. *(gathering her resolve)* Listen. Hamel. Are you aware that…

HAMEL. Hey, kid. Where'd you put my turquoise shirt?

DOTTY. *(to the audience)* Not the turquoise shirt!

HAMEL. Where the fuck is it?

DOTTY. The second drawer. Hamel, last night, I looked in your pocket and…When the roses came I thought… And then this phone call from a….

*(**HAMEL** strides through in his turquoise shirt. He throws **DOTTY** his uniform.)*

HAMEL. Wash this, would ya?

DOTTY. Hamel…

HAMEL. Don't leave the apartment, Kid.

DOTTY. Hamel. Dear.

HAMEL. Like my papa always said, *"Don't leave the apartment."* *(click click)* Later.

(He is gone.

DOTTY looks in the pocket. She finds another picture. She looks on the back. A wave of nausea hits her.)

(LIGHT SHIFT)

(A sign drops down – "ZENA's Beauty Emporium." DOTTY enters terrified.)

DOTTY. Here I am outside Zena's Beauty Emporium. I feel certain that there's been some huge mix-up, don't you? Like my Mama always said, "Don't believe what you see, believe what you're told!"

(She knocks timidly on the door.)

I'm sure this Zena is a lovely person and her connection with my husband is purely innocent and we'll all have a hearty laugh about this soon!

(She gives the audience a brave wink and a hopeful, winning smile.

The door bursts violently open and ZENA's head appears. She is furious.)

ZENA. Keep ya friggin pants on!!! I'm tryin ta meditate here! Christ!

(She disappears inside and slams the door behind her.)

DOTTY. Mama also said, "Keep your head in the sand and you won't get a sunburn!"

(She begins to slink away when the door opens again and ZENA comes out. She now has the poised and elegant air of the proprietress of Zena's Beauty Emporium. Even the faint scent of Britain mingles with the Bronx.)

ZENA. Mrs. Cuthbert. So sorry to keep you waiting, but if I don't give my meditation it's due, I frown, and with frowns comes wrinkles. Such is the way with spirituality! You *are* a tad early. Please, come in.

DOTTY. Actually, I'm not Mrs....

ZENA. *(cutting her off)* No no, of course not. The customer is always right. If you say you're not early, *I'm* the moron.

DOTTY. No. I was just…I'm not actually Mrs…

ZENA. *(rapid fire, without a breath)* Now, I have you down for just a manicure today, Mrs. Cuthbert, peach passion I'm thinking with your delicate coloring, but as a new customer to Zena's Beauty Emporium, you are also entitled to 25% off our spring-into-spring facial.

DOTTY. No, I'm not…I actually came to talk to you about my husb…

ZENA. Of course, here at Zena's Beauty Emporium there is no sales pressure, and absolutely no obligation for you, the customer, to improve yourself in areas that you are not yet prepared to improve.

DOTTY. I think there's been a mistake.

ZENA. *(quietly furious) Fine. No facial. No sweat off my nose.*

(A manicure table and two chairs appear.)

SIT!

(DOTTY *does.* **ZENA** *takes out a bowl of soaking solution.)*

Soak.

DOTTY. No, really. I need to…

ZENA. SOAK!!!!

(DOTTY *plunges her hands into the solution.*

Zena's charm returns)

You're probably surprised that Zena herself is acting as manicurist.

DOTTY. Well, I didn't…

ZENA. *(Grabbing* **DOTTY***'s hand from the solution and filing furiously.)* I was forced this morning to fire my third assistant this week. When you're a perfectionist in the beauty industry…

DOTTY. Ow!!

ZENA. *Don't move and you won't get hurt!* When you're a perfectionist as I am, it's very hard to tolerate incompetence or insubordination. Now, about the facial…

DOTTY. The thing is...

ZENA. How would you like that dry, age-pocked skin to glow like the day you were twenty-four?

DOTTY. But I'm twenty-three.

ZENA. You're *twenty-three?!*

DOTTY. Yes.

ZENA. You're twenty-three.

DOTTY. Yes.

ZENA. Jesus.

DOTTY. Why?

ZENA. Please, let's just continue with your nails.

(*She takes* **DOTTY***'s other hand and begins filing.*)

DOTTY. Does my skin...Is there something wrong with my face? Am I...

ZENA. May I ask you something of a personal nature?

DOTTY. Uhhh...Yes?

ZENA. How do you cleanse your face? Epoxy?

DOTTY. Epoxy?

ZENA. Sulfuric acid? Or maybe you just take a little sandpaper and rub it on your face?

DOTTY. Oh no! I use soap.

(**ZENA** *gasps, stricken.*)

Is that...is that wrong? Should I...

ZENA. May I ask you another personal question?

DOTTY. Uhhh...

ZENA. Do you *hate* your face?

DOTTY. Hate my...no. No, I...

ZENA. Strengthener?

DOTTY. Huh?

ZENA. Two dollars extra. I'm doing you a favor. Believe me.

(*She begins applying the nail strengthener.*)

Now, I'm not telling you what you should do...

DOTTY. No! Please, tell me. See, where I come from, we wash with soap. I didn't...what should I be...

ZENA. *(A bottle appears.)* Zena's Beauty Cream. Look at my face. Closer. Do you see any pores?

DOTTY. What's a pore?

ZENA. Exactly. And you know what did that?

DOTTY. Zena's Beauty Cream?

ZENA. I'm sorry, you said the peach passion?

DOTTY. Well, I don't know. Do you think, with my...

ZENA. I'm going to apply the nail strengthener, two coats of peach passion, a hardening agent, and a layer of sheen. Your nails are disgusting. It's a miracle they haven't broken off down to the stem. I'm nauseated looking at them, I really am.

DOTTY. Oh my!

ZENA. Now hold very still. Don't even breathe.

> *(**DOTTY** holds her breath as **ZENA** works.)*

Shall I put you down for a 16 ounce bottle or the 32?

DOTTY. Well, I don't...How much does it...

ZENA. We can discuss this while you're drying.

DOTTY. In fact, how much did you say my nails were going to...

ZENA. Mrs. Cuthbert, can you really put a price tag on your appearance?

DOTTY. Gee, I guess not...

> *(The door opens and **DAN**, dressed as **MRS. CUTHBERT**, an elegant older woman, enters.)*

ZENA. No off-the-streets. Call for an appointment.

DAN. I beg your pardon, I have an appointment. Mrs. Eugenia Cuthbert here for my 11:30 manicure.

DOTTY. Oh dear.

ZENA. *(to **DAN**)* Look, Lady, I don't know what friggin' game you're playin', but this here

> *(indicating **DOTTY**)*

is Mrs Cuth....

DOTTY. No, wait. See, there's been a mix-up. I'm not actually Mrs. Cuthbert. I'm...

ZENA. *What????*

DOTTY. I was trying to tell you. I'm not Mrs. Cuthbert. I came here today to talk to you about…

ZENA. I'm sitting here like an a-hole, excuse me, Mrs. Cuthbert, giving you priceless tips on beauty management, and you're not Mrs. Cuthbert???

DOTTY. Please…it's all a terrible…

ZENA. *Out of my Emporium!!!*

DOTTY. I'm so sorry…I…

ZENA. You pay me and get the hell out of here. And no 25 percent bullshit for you.

DAN. Oh my!

DOTTY. Please. I only have…

ZENA. With the strengthener it's $7.76. Ten dollars even with the tip.

DOTTY. See, I was trying to tell you…I only have a dollar thirty-seven.

(She starts to reach into her pocket and then remembers her nails.)

If you could just reach in…I don't want to get my lovely nails…

ZENA. You don't even have the money????

*(She grabs **DOTTY** by the collar with one hand and begins lifting her off the ground.)*

You come in here passing yourself off as Mrs. Cuthbert…

DAN. *(very alarmed, rushing from the shop)* Heavens!

ZENA. *(dropping **DOTTY**)* No! Mrs. Cuthbert! Wait!

*(But **MRS. CUTHBERT** is gone. Turning on **DOTTY**)*

You rat. You scum. Not only do you try to cheat me outta ten bucks, you lose me my client. What should I do to you?

DOTTY. If I could explain…

ZENA. I should call the cops.

DOTTY. No! Please. I'm not supposed to be out of the apartment!

ZENA. I should perm your hair till it falls out in clumps!

DOTTY. No!

ZENA. I should apply the tightener without the relaxant!

DOTTY. No, please!

ZENA. I should, but I'm just too goddammned sweet. It's my tragic flaw, it really is.

DOTTY. Oh, thank you so much! I wish I could repay you, but…

ZENA. Oh, no. You're gonna repay me. Believe you me. Let's see…the nails and Mrs. Cuthbert should tally up to about a week's worth of slave labor. Be here tomorrow ten A.M. You're my new assistant.

DOTTY. Me? In the beauty business?

ZENA. Now, amscray before I change my mind and just exfoliate you.

DOTTY. Oh thank you. Thank you so much!

ZENA. *Out!!!*

> (**ZENA***'s Beauty Emporium flies off.*
>
> **DOTTY** *turns to the audience, exuberant.*)

DOTTY. Me, a beauty care provider??? I think my head might explode!

> (*She takes a moment to try to take this all in.*)

Isn't she remarkable? Zena. She's the most remarkable person I ever met. Such confidence. Such sophistication. And she's so beautiful and smart and – did you see her nails??? Everything about her was perfect.

> (*relieved and delighted now*)

Well! I feel more certain than ever I was wrong. What would a woman like Zena possibly see in my Hamel? Like my Mama always said, "You won't see a swan mounting a duck!"

> (*LIGHT SHIFT*
>
> *A toilet appears.* **DOTTY** *is on her hands and knees before it scrubbing the floor with a toothbrush, cheerily humming "I'm a Little Tea Pot."*
>
> *We hear* **ZENA** *yell from offstage.*)

ZENA. When you finish the bathroom, start in on the clos-
ets. And hurry up, it's almost closing!

(The phone rings.)

DOTTY. Right you are, Chief! Should I do the coat closet or
just the...

ZENA. Shut up! I'm on the phone here. Christ!

DOTTY. Oky-doke!

(She looks up and sees us.)

Hey! Here I am at Zena's Beauty Emporium, cleaning
the bathroom floors with a toothbrush! The week has
just flown by. Like my Mama always said, "There's a
special room in heaven for girls who clean toilets!"

ZENA. *(From offstage. Her voice reverberates with a God-like,
booming tone.* DOTTY *looks up and out to address her.)* Hey!
You!

DOTTY. Yes, Zena?

ZENA. *(entering)* You still want that facial?

DOTTY. Me? Want a personal beauty treatment by...

ZENA. You want it or not?

DOTTY. Yes!!! Oh, yes! Of course!

(to us)

It just gets better and better!

ZENA. Monday morning Mrs. Peabody is comin in for "the
works." Head to toe glamour. It's a two-man job. I need
someone to pedicure while I perm, moisturize while I
exfoliate, wax while I pluck.

DOTTY. Are you still talking about the floors?

ZENA. You're obviously not the ideal choice. In fact, you're
the bottom of the barrel, but you're pliable and
cheap.

DOTTY. Wow. Thanks!

ZENA. You look like crap. Here in Zena's Beauty Emporium
there's no looking like crap in the client's presence.
So take care of that before Monday.

DOTTY. What should I...

ZENA. Here's this month's "Beautiful or Bust."

(*A magazine falls to* DOTTY*'s feet from the ceiling.*)

Memorize the article on page 57.

DOTTY. *(thumbs through and finds the article)* "How to Kiss Up to Your Hard-to-Please Female Employer." Yowza!

ZENA. Now get the hell outta here. I'm off to Atlantic City for the weekend.

DOTTY. Yes, Ma'am!

(*She gets up and begins to leave.*)

ZENA. Hey. What's your name anyway?

DOTTY. Well, my proper name is Dorothea, but...

ZENA. Sucks. No je ne'sais qua. I hate it. Your new name is...Peaches.

DOTTY. Peaches???

ZENA. It'll give you something to aspire to.

DOTTY. Wow! A goal!

ZENA. Now scram.

DOTTY. Yes, Ma'am!

(LIGHTS SHIFT)

(**DOTTY** *is outside the shop, looking at the magazine cover with her mouth agape.*)

Holy Moly! You should see this girl! Her dress is down to here and there's a slit up to there, and you can see almost everything in between.

(She thinks.)

Why would ladies want to look at these pictures? Maybe they just buy it for the articles.

(LIGHT SHIFT)

(**DOTTY**'s *kitchen table.* **HAMEL** *is sitting with his feet up on the table, reading "Service Station Weekly" and eating cheese doodles.* **DOTTY** *is working on an extravagant papier-mache model of a toilet, and climbing the walls.*)

DOTTY. Hamel is here!

(She looks at him with misery and disbelief.)

It's Sunday afternoon and I haven't had a second to memorize "Beautiful or Bust" or to work on not looking like crap.

HAMEL. Hey, Kid?

DOTTY. Yes, Hamel Dear?

HAMEL. You know what would go good with these doodles?

DOTTY. No, Sweetheart.

HAMEL. A brew.

DOTTY. Good thinking, Hamel!

(to the audience)

Ever since I've been out of the apartment, when I'm in it seems so small. And Hamel takes up so much of it. There's barely enough air in here for the both of us.

HAMEL. Hey! The beer!

(She grabs one and hands it to him.)

DOTTY. Here, Hamel Dear. Whenever he goes to the bathroom I try to sneak glimpses of "Beautiful or Bust," but I'm just not a quick reader. Oh, what will I do tomorrow? What will I wear? What does exfoliate mean?

HAMEL. *(looks up as if suddenly he heard that)* Huh?

DOTTY. What?

HAMEL. Whatchu say?

DOTTY. Oh, nothing…

HAMEL. *(noticing the toilet for the first time)* Hey.

DOTTY. What?

HAMEL. Hey.

DOTTY. Yes, Dear?

HAMEL. What the hell is that?

DOTTY. This?

HAMEL. What the hell you makin there?

DOTTY. Umm…this is papier-mache, Hamel Dear.

HAMEL. What is it?

DOTTY. It's...ummm, it's a commode.

HAMEL. It's a toilet.

DOTTY. Yes, that's right. A toilet.

HAMEL. That's a toilet.

DOTTY. Yes.

HAMEL. Whose toilet is that?

DOTTY. It's...It's our toilet, Hamel Dear.

HAMEL. That ain't our toilet.

DOTTY. It is...

HAMEL. Do I look like an idiot to you?

DOTTY. Well...

HAMEL. Whose toilet is that?

DOTTY. It's...

HAMEL. You're doin' someone else's toilet!

DOTTY. No. No, this...

HAMEL. Where you seen someone else's toilet?

DOTTY. I didn't! I just...

HAMEL. You been out of the apartment? You been out seeing other people's toilets?

DOTTY. No! No, I...It's...It's from...from my memory! It's from my memory! Of a toilet...Of a toilet from...from when I grew up. That's it. It's my childhood toilet.

(to the audience)

Oh my lord! I'm lying! I've never lied to Hamel before! And I'm so good at it! Oh my lord!!!!

HAMEL. Oh.

DOTTY. Yes. It's my childhood toilet!

HAMEL. Oh. Okay.

DOTTY. Yes.

HAMEL. I like it. It's good.

DOTTY. Thank you Hamel.

HAMEL. You should do some more. Toilets. It's good.

DOTTY. All right, Dear! I will! Thank you, Dear.

*(**HAMEL** returns to his magazine.)*

He liked it! Hamel's never noticed any of my artwork before. Not even the mosaic of our bathroom sink, my best effort, I think.

(She considers the toilet.)

I wonder what he sees in this toilet?

(She thinks.)

Has Hamel suddenly become an aesthete?

HAMEL. *(holding up the empty bag)* Hey, Kid, you got more doodles?

DOTTY. Yes, Dear!

(She lifts some debris from the table and finds another bag of cheese doodles.)

Or is it *me?* Is there something different about me now that I've left the apartment and seen other toilets?

I feel different. About this apartment. About Hamel. About everything. And when I'm walking to Zena's Beauty Emporium, and I pass by other people, I want to see their toilets. Their refrigerators, their sinks, their kitchen tables. I have a curiosity about things I never had before. A hunger. A yearning. So many questions. And I just know the answers are in "Beautiful or Bust" if Hamel ever leaves so I can read it!!!!!!

HAMEL. Hey Kid, think I'll go out. You need anything?

DOTTY. Oh, thank you Lord!

HAMEL. Huh?

DOTTY. Umm, yes! I need more construction paper. And finger paints and glitter and paste and tape.

HAMEL. How bout that stuff you made the toilet with? Can I get you mora that?

DOTTY. I could use some more flour to make the paste!

HAMEL. You betcha. I sure do like that toilet.

DOTTY. Oh, and Hamel, Dear?

HAMEL. Yeah?

DOTTY. Could you get me some hair spray?

HAMEL. Huh?

DOTTY. To...to help for my...my...it's ummm...for my papier-mache...eh...to dry?

(to us)

My! I'm an artful deceiver. I'm shocked at my aptitude for duplicity and guile. And now that my true nature has surfaced, there's no knowing the level of chicanery I'm capable of! Heavens!

HAMEL. You got it.

(He kisses her on the forehead.)

See ya, Kid. Like my Papa always said, *"Don't leave the apartment."*

(He's gone.)

DOTTY. Bye, Dear!

(She dives for her magazine as the lights fade.)

Holy Moly!

(There is a flash of lightning, the crash of thunder and the sound of rain.

*We see **DOTTY** rushing to work. She is soaked to the skin, her hair plastered to her head, clutching "Beautiful or Bust" and muttering to herself, We hear ghostly voices amidst the rain and thunder.)*

VOICES. Anti-oxidants.

Pore refining cleanser.

Volumizing, replenishing and balancing.

Time released moisturizers.

Alpha and Beta Hydroxys with gentle micro beads.

Naturally derived polymer.

Rich in vitamins for visible radiance.

DOTTY. *(under the voices)* Mood boosting perfumes. Tooth whitening. The natural renewal process. Energizing, anti-fatigue, holistic, luminosity-intensifying, volume replenishing...Holy Moly!

(She races off.)

(ZENA's Beauty Emporium. There is lightning, thunder and rain, reminiscent of Dr. Frankenstein's lab. MRS. PEABODY [DAN] is stretched out in the beautician's chair reading "Dazzling Divorcee" magazine. We cannot see her face or hair. ZENA is hard at work as MRS. PEABODY talks.)

DAN. So I said to him, Elsworth, if that's how you want it, you can pack your bags and there's the door.

ZENA. Good fa you, Honey. Turn.

DAN. And he said, But Sweetheart, how could you throw away forty years of marriage, our house, our cars, our equity?

ZENA. No, turn this way.

DAN. And I said, Elsworth, you take the forty years, I'll take the rest.

ZENA. Beautiful. Don't move.

(DOTTY bursts in dripping wet.)

DOTTY. I'm so terribly sorry I'm late, Zena. I spent two hours giving my hair ample voluminosity but then it started raining, and I don't have an umbrella, and...

ZENA. Excuse me, Mrs. Peabody.

(She rushes at DOTTY in a fury, hissing like a broken boiler.)

What in the hell?! You look like a wet pig! I can't have the client see you like this!

DOTTY. I'm so very, very sorry, Zena, but...

ZENA. *Clam it!!!!* Go put on the ensemble hanging in the back room. Pronto. I need you on Mrs. Peabody's feet. *Now!!!!*

DOTTY. Great! Thanks! Sorry again about this. Thanks!

ZENA. *NOW!!!!!!*

(DOTTY rushes off and ZENA returns to MRS. PEABODY.)

Aright, Mrs. Peabody. My assistant will begin your pedicure in a moment. Why don't you begin soaking and I'll get to work on your face.

(She puts **MRS. PEABODY**'s *feet in a basin of water and begins applying a green paste to her face.)*

DAN. Then I made kissy kissy and when he left for his Sunday golf league, I had all the locks changed.

ZENA. Beautiful. Always change the locks first. Well, the bank accounts and then the locks. I learned the hard way, believe you me. With the first two, I was an idiot and came away with nyet.

*(**DOTTY** comes rushing back in wearing a leopard skin jumpsuit that hangs in all the wrong places and a matching leopard skin turban.)*

DOTTY. Here I am! All set to beautify!

ZENA. Dry Mrs. Peabody's feet, Peaches. And then start painting. The kissable coral.

DOTTY. With your coloring, the kissable coral is an exquisite, radiant, replenishing, moisturizing, beta hydroxizing choice, Mrs. Peabody!

ZENA. Paint, Peaches!

DOTTY. You betcha!

(She gets to work during the following, but is quickly finished.)

ZENA. The first two husbands were a nightmare. The next three I made out like a bandit. In fact, Zena's Beauty Emporium is a monument to my gains.

DOTTY. Holy Cow!!! You had *five* husbands?!

ZENA. Paint, Peaches. Don't talk.

DOTTY. Right. Sorry.

(under her breath)

Holy cow. *Five husbands?* Holy cow.

DAN. Are you married now, Dear?

ZENA. Right now I'm between husbands. But of course, I'm looking to change that. I very much believe in the sanctity of marriage.

DAN. Oh, so do I.

ZENA. I've got number six on the hook. Just got to reel him in.

DOTTY. You do? What's his name?

ZENA. No one you'd know, Peaches.

DOTTY. Oh, Zena, please tell me. Does it start with an "H"?

ZENA. *Paint, Peaches.*

DAN. Oh, now, don't be so coy, Dear. I want to hear all about this dark stranger too!

ZENA. *(A growl of a sigh. With looks to kill at* DOTTY*)* I call him Derk.

DOTTY. Derk!!! His name is Derk? I knew it!

(She rushes at ZENA *and throws her arms around her neck.)*

Oh, Zena! That's so wonderful! I hope you're very very very happy.

DAN. Isn't that sweet!

ZENA. Get off me and get back to Mrs. Peabody's feet, Peaches.

DOTTY. *(She has finished the first coat and doesn't know what to do.)* I did the kissable coral, Zena. Should I...

ZENA. Keep painting!

DOTTY. Anything in particular or...

ZENA. Excuse me, Mrs. Peabody.

(She lifts DOTTY *and moves her across the room.)*

Look, Peaches. My repartee with the clientele is 73 and three quarters percent of the business. You keep talkin', you keep interruptin', you keep jumping on me like a *freak*, all I got is 26 and a quarter left to maneuver, kapich? When I say paint, you paint.

DOTTY. Great! I love to paint!

ZENA. *Paint.*

(They both return to their positions, DOTTY *choosing colors and painting madly.)*

Now, this is going to start to harden, Mrs. Peabody, so you shouldn't move your face too much.

DAN. I did want to discuss my cosmetic make-over with you.

ZENA. Ya better talk fast cause soon your mouth's not gonna move so good.

DAN. I feel that makeup should not conceal, but instead highlight the wholesome, down-to-earth, homey aspect of my countenance.

ZENA. Wholesome and homey. You got it.

DAN. While still emphasizing my best feature, the eyes.

ZENA. Windows to the soul.

DAN. Perhaps with a sea foam eye shadow with a metallic blue liner.

ZENA. I hear ya, Mrs. P.

DOTTY. I'm done!

ZENA. Excellent. Your nails are drying, your face is hardening, your highlights are setting. Why don't you sit up slowly and proceed to the drying, hardening, setting area of the emporium.

> (**MRS. PEABODY** *sits up. Her face is covered in green goop and her hair is twisted into those little aluminum foil things. There is a flash of lightning and a crack of thunder.* **DOTTY** *sees her and shrieks in terror.* **MRS. PEABODY** *shrieks in return.*)

DOTTY. Holy Crow! What happened to your face???

DAN. *(looking down)* Lordy day! What happened to my feet???

ZENA. Oh crap!!!

DOTTY. I painted them. I didn't know what to do exactly, but I heard you talking about your wholesomeness and the homey aspect to your radiant splendiforousness, so there it is.

DAN. What *is* that???

DOTTY. Well, here's my refrigerator, on the big toes. Needed a lot of room for that. And then on the pinky toes I put my toaster – the pop-up stopped working, but it's still mighty handsome. In the middle, that's Zena's toilet, which happens to be particularly lovely. On the ring toe, I decided to...

ZENA. THAT'S *IT* PEACHES!!! YOU'RE...

DAN. Brilliant!

ZENA. Brilliant?

DOTTY. Huh?

DAN. This is brilliant. I love them. You have captured the essence of domesticity and brought to light my appreciation of life's simplicity and grace. Can you do my fingernails as well?

DOTTY. Well, I never tried, but…

ZENA. Of course she can. Peaches does an extensive array of appliance nail art.

DAN. Fabulous! You are a find. Look, the annual mah jong tourny is this weekend, and I know my friends Mrs. Frankenwaller and Mrs. Le Pieu will want you to work on them as well. I imagine you're booked solid for tomorrow but…

ZENA. Let me check the book.

(She goes to do so.)

Ah! Peaches happens to have an opening at noon today and…

DOTTY. But, Zena. I'm supposed to finish cleaning the floors with a toothbrush at noon!

ZENA. Is that a riot? All that talent and a sense of humor. As I was saying, I have two free spots tomorrow morning. Shall I pencil in your friends?

DAN. Fantastic!

ZENA. Marvelous.

DOTTY. Wow.

ZENA. Peaches, I'm going to make Mrs. Peabody comfortable. You go put your feet up! Relax a little. Help yourself to one of our complimentary lattes!

DOTTY. Wow. A latte. I'm not sure what that is, but it certainly sounds…

(A sudden wave of nausea.)

Oops. I think I'm gonna be sick!

(She rushes off.

Rushes into her apartment. **HAMEL** *is standing in the middle of the floor, stupefied.)*

Hamel!

HAMEL. You…weren't….here.

DOTTY. Hamel!

HAMEL. You weren't here.

DOTTY. Hamel! Hamel…I

HAMEL. I came in.

DOTTY. Yes, Hamel?

HAMEL. I opened the door and came in and said *(click click)*, "Hey, Kid."

DOTTY. Right.

HAMEL. Just like I always do.

DOTTY. I know you do Hamel. I know you always tend to do that.

HAMEL. And every time I do that, every time I open the door and come in and say *(click click)* "Hey Kid," there you are. There you are where you always are and where you're always supposed to be.

DOTTY. Right. Of course.

HAMEL. But today I come in. I open the door. I say *(click click)* "Hey Kid" and nothin happens.

DOTTY. No?

HAMEL. Nothin' happens because you're not here.

DOTTY. No. Well…

HAMEL. And then I'm standing here…I'm standing here stupefied…

DOTTY. Yes, Hamel. I can see that.

HAMEL. And *you* walk in. *I'm* the one who's supposed to walk in. Not you. You're supposed to be here.

DOTTY. Hamel. What happened was…

HAMEL. And here you are, you're dressed like some wild game hunter from India or something.

DOTTY. Ah! Yes. There's an excellent explanation, Hamel, Dear.

HAMEL. Well, I would love to hear it. I'm salivating at the mouth to hear this excellent explanation. Cause I'm tellin you right now, with what I see and hear so far, I'm not too happy. Not too happy at all.

DOTTY. Ok. Well, see, Hamel. I was…I was…

HAMEL. Yeah?

DOTTY. …downstairs…

HAMEL. Are you supposed to be downstairs?

DOTTY. In the laundry room!

HAMEL. Dressed like a wild game hunter from India?

DOTTY. Ah! No. No, I was in my house dress…

HAMEL. Right…

DOTTY. And I put the wash in.

HAMEL. Yes.

DOTTY. And I notice that my house dress really could use a good washing. And and and…there's this leopard skin jumpsuit with matching turban, just sitting there on top of the dryer like someone forgot it there…

HAMEL. Right.

DOTTY. So, quick as a little bunny, I slip on the jumpsuit so I could put my dress in the wash! And that's why it took me longer and that's why I wasn't here when you came in, and that's why I'm wearing this leopard skin jumpsuit and matching turban! That's it! That's the excellent explanation!

HAMEL. *(Long pause. Then, completely satisfied)* Oh. Okay.

DOTTY. Yes! That's it!

HAMEL. What's for dinner?

DOTTY. I'll have your smiley-face burger ready in two shakes of a lamb's tail, Hamel Dear!

HAMEL. Aright. I'll be in the can.

(He leaves.)

DOTTY. *(to us)* Wow, I'm good.

(ZENA's Beauty Emporium. DOTTY is still in the leopard skin jumpsuit, but now she has a white towel wrapped around her head.)

What a day I've had! All day long ladies came in to get toilets and such on their finger and toe nails. And now Zena is going to give me my facial! And she wants me to keep coming back! Somebody pinch me, this can't be happening!

ZENA. *(The facial chair and a bowl of green goop appear.)* Alright Peaches. Assume the position.

DOTTY. A beautifying treatment – for *me!*

ZENA. Hurry it up.

> (**DOTTY** *hops in the chair and* **ZENA** *slings a beauty-parlor drape over her.*)
>
> I gotta be quick here. My beau is comin to take me out to Jimmy's Hideaway. I got the feelin tonight is the night.
>
> *(She beings applying muck to* **DOTTY***'s face.)*

DOTTY. The night?

ZENA. I think he's gonna pop the question.

DOTTY. The question?

ZENA. Ask me to marry him, Peaches. Sheesh.

DOTTY. Oh, Zena! How thrilling!

ZENA. Yeah. And then it's Aloha, Las Vegas.

DOTTY. My!

ZENA. There's only one minor hitch.

DOTTY. What's that?

ZENA. His wife.

DOTTY. He's married? Then how can he…

ZENA. A minor inconvenience. She's a total loser. He'll gladly dump her like a bin of recyclables for me.

DOTTY. Gosh! What's wrong with her?

ZENA. Well, from what he says, she's not a real woman.

DOTTY. Wow. What is she?

ZENA. Sounds like a freak. She doesn't know how to dress, she doesn't know how to look, she doesn't know how to act.

DOTTY. Poor thing!

ZENA. A total zero. I can't imagine why he married her and neither can he. But it's all just a technicality now. As soon as I get the rock on my finger, she's history.

DOTTY. Gee, Zena. Don't you feel a little funny going out with a married man? I mean, aren't there moral and ethical issues that…

ZENA. Let me tell you something, Peaches. I used to have moral and ethical issues comin out my ass. And then suddenly Diana was gone and I realized I got to grab the world by the short hairs and run with it, you know?

DOTTY. Diana?

ZENA. Hit me like a ton of bricks. Stopped eating, sleeping, waxing my inner thighs. Basically, I gave up on life. Don't move your face so much, you got to let the undercoat set.

DOTTY. *(moving her face less)* Who was Diana? Your sister?

ZENA. What?

DOTTY. Your Mom? Your cat?

ZENA. No, idiot! Princess Diana.

DOTTY. Oh my gosh, did she die?

ZENA. What do you, live in a cave?

DOTTY. I don't get out much.

ZENA. Diana. It's like we were separated at birth or something. She was a princess; I was Miss Tri-borough Area. She was a simple girl with an illustrious, high-profile marriage; my wedding at the Seafood Suaree was covered in three local papers. We shared the same subdued but elegant taste in clothes and jewelry. We were like soul mates who had never met.

DOTTY. Soul mates. Golly.

ZENA. Naturally I took it hard. But after three months of mourning, I awoke with a new zest for living and the revelation that I must carpe diem.

DOTTY. Jeepers. What's that?

ZENA. It's Latin. It means, don't give a shit for anybody or anything, but go after what you want with the bloodthirsty vengeance of a wolverine in heat.

DOTTY. Wow. You speak Latin.

ZENA. And my life has never been the same. I went through husband number five, acquired the Emporium and it's been Zena's time in the sun ever since. You're done. You can sit up.

(She cranks up the chair. **DOTTY** *is covered in green goop.)*

Just don't move your face.

(looking at her watch)

Christ! That bastard's three minutes late. I'm gonna fry his ass.

DOTTY. Is this new fella rich too, Zena?

ZENA. No. This one's just good in bed. He needs a lot of work in every other area, but I've already made some significant changes and once I have him under my complete control…

*(***HAMEL*** *rushes in.)*

DOTTY. *(not moving her mouth)* Holy smokes!

HAMEL. Zena, baby. I just got out…I'm real sorry. I…

ZENA. You're late!

(She slaps him across the face, three times, hard. He grabs her and dips her into a passionate Hollywood kiss. **DOTTY** *sits, dumbfounded.)*

HAMEL. *(seeing* **DOTTY** *but, of course, not recognizing her)* Oh, scuse me ma'am.

ZENA. Derk, this is my assistant, Peaches. Peaches, Derk.

HAMEL. How do?

DOTTY. *(barely able to speak)* Derk? *You're* Derk?

ZENA. Had a God-awful name when I met him. Derk suits him much better.

HAMEL. If Zena says it's true, it must be true.

(He takes a dozen roses from his back pocket and presents them to her on one knee.)

Flowers for the most beautiful flower on earth.

ZENA. What am I supposed to do with these?

HAMEL. Uhhh…

ZENA. Here.

(She throws them to **DOTTY**.*)*

We're gonna split. You
hour. Your face is gonna
it's covered in a million l.
all directions. That means
begun. When the pain is re
can't take it any more, wait ten
crack the stuff off. Ciao, baby.

HAMEL. Nice to meet you, Peaches.

*(He scoops **ZENA** up in his arms and*

DOTTY *sits dumbfounded for several* ___ *. Then streams of tears begin cutting streaks through her green face.)*

DOTTY. *(her mouth still barely able to move)* It's my Hamel. It's my Hamel she's after. And he's not even my Hamel any more. He's Derk.

(She sits for a moment, letting it all sink in.)

Not a real woman. A loser. A freak. Doesn't know how to dress, how to look, how to act. That's *me* they were talking about. A zero. They mean me. How could I have not known this? How did the fact that I'm a freak and a loser and not even a real woman escape me?

(She comes down to the audience.)

Did you know? Have you known all this time, watched me chirping around like a fool being happy and hope-ful, have you sat there in your comfortable seats and thought all these things about me, that I was a loser, that I was not really a woman, have you thought all that and not even said a word to me about it?

(She looks around the audience.)

You all look like real women to me. Well, not you men of course. But you women. You all look much closer to those magazine ladies than I do.

What's wrong with me? How did I not notice all this before? I was so happy. I was such a fool.

(Suddenly, her face starts feeling like a million little sand crabs pulling it in all directions.)

...face feels like a million little sand crabs pull-
...all directions. OWWWW. I have to get it off!

(She grabs a towel, and then remembers.)

No! This means the beautifying process is starting. Now I'm supposed to wait. Geez. It hurts so much. Oww. My face.

(She sits and begins to wait. Weeping)

This beautifying is really really hard and painful. I don't know if I've got what it takes.

(She grabs her copy of "Beautiful or Bust" and stares at the woman on the front cover. She then takes a little mirror and looks at her own green reflection.)

And I have such a long way to go. Owww.

(A sudden wave of nausea.)

And I think I'm going to be sick. Scuse me.

(She runs off.)

(BLACKOUT)

End of Act I

ACT II

(Zena's Beauty Emporium

DOTTY *enters. She is still wearing the leopard skin jumpsuit and has all but destroyed the ozone layer with hair spray.*

She has used bright, primary-color finger paints to highlight her features. Bright red circles on her cheeks and mouth, bright blue eye shadow all the way up to thick brown eyebrows.

Heartbroken, she is still trying very hard to be brave and cheery. She also adopts **ZENA***'s elegant beautician tone.)*

DOTTY. Zena! I've arrived!

ZENA. Your first client's not 'till ten so you got…

(entering)

Holy shit, what happened to you?!

DOTTY. *(a bit shaken by this)* Whatever do you mean?

ZENA. Did somebody beat the crap out of you or something? Jesus. You look like hell.

DOTTY. *(weepy)* I do?

ZENA. Who did this to you? I'll kill him.

DOTTY. *(wailing)* I did it to me!!!

ZENA. *You* did it? Are you drunk?

DOTTY. I was working on not looking like crap! I was beautifying, like in the magazine.

ZENA. What magazine? Creature Features?

DOTTY. Ohhhhhhh! I can't do anything right!

(She collapses to the floor, sobbing. **ZENA** *goes to comfort her, but can't bring herself to actually make physical contact.)*

ZENA. Peaches, pull yourself together. We can fix this. Please.

DOTTY. No. It's impossible. I'm a freak.

ZENA. Hey, hey. Come on now. You're not exactly a freak.

DOTTY. It's hopeless. I'm a loser.

(She looks up. Her tears have streaked the paints into a colorful mishmash.)

ZENA. Well...You're a challenge, I'll give you that. But anyone can be improved. We just need to set some realistic goals. What is that on your face?

DOTTY. Finger paints. It's all I have.

ZENA. Okay, now that's a beauty don't. Here. Come here.

(She puts **DOTTY** *in the beauty chair and throws her a towel.)*

Uh, clean yourself up a little, okay? I'll get some product.

(A beauty tray of product appears, while **DOTTY** *cleans off her face.* **ZENA** *throws the beauty coverall over her.)*

There's a lot to do. We gotta work fast here.

DOTTY. *(with the leftover hiccups of crying)* Th-th-thanks, Zena.

ZENA. No more crying, you'll mess up my work.

DOTTY. O-O-Ok.

*(***ZENA** *applies product rapid-fire.)*

ZENA. What the hell started all this, Peaches? You're always so irritatingly cheery. It was your one good feature. When you got a positive feature like that, try not to fuck with it, all right?

DOTTY. *(trying to be cheerful)* All right.

ZENA. So, what brought this on?

DOTTY. *(wailing again)* My...my...my...husband loves another woman!!!

ZENA. Christ! You're married?

DOTTY. Yes.

ZENA. Someone married you?

DOTTY. Yes.

ZENA. And now he's fooling around?

DOTTY. Yeeesss!!!

ZENA. Let's cut his nuts off!

DOTTY. No.

ZENA. No? Let's get a good lawyer, then. Take this creep for everything he's got!

DOTTY. No.

ZENA. *No?* Then…let's cut his nuts off!

DOTTY. No.

ZENA. *No?* Geez, Peaches, I'm runnin out of ideas here.

DOTTY. I love him. I want him back.

ZENA. Crap. What's the other chick like?

DOTTY. She's beautiful and cultured and confident and she has lots and lots of sex appeal.

ZENA. *(beat)* You sure we can't just cut his nuts off?

DOTTY. No.

ZENA. Aright. We'll win him back. Shit. We got a lot of work ahead of us, but we'll see what we can do.

DOTTY. Really??? Oh, Zena, thank you!!!

(She throws herself at **ZENA.***)*

ZENA. Yeah, the first thing is, none of that. I got no use for physical contact with women, you know?

DOTTY. Oh. Okay. Sorry.

ZENA. Now, hold still, I'm giving you some facial structure.

DOTTY. Okay!

ZENA. You can't keep wearing this outfit a mine. Our customers expect a change of scenery. You got anything else?

DOTTY. This is the most elegant thing I have.

ZENA. I got some stuff in the back I can loan you. We're gonna have to work on your body. You got a very strange shape to you, Peaches. You're flat as a boy, and then suddenly you got this…well…thick waist. You're gonna have to compensate with huge boobs.

DOTTY. How do I do that?

ZENA. I got a wide array of shapes and sizes in the back. I think we'll add some hips too to compensate for your huge gut. You really gotta watch what you eat, Peaches.

DOTTY. I don't know what it is. All of a sudden I'm just getting bigger and bigger. What do I do?

ZENA. You could try exercising. But that never works. Starving yourself is really the best way. And if you do eat, throw it right back up.

DOTTY. I'm really good at that!

ZENA. Great. And fill up on coffee and saccarin, that's what I do.

DOTTY. OK.

ZENA. Really commit yourself to the magazines. They'll help you in every area. And then, before you say or do anything stupid, stop and ask yourself, "What would those women in the magazines do in this situation?"

DOTTY. Right.

ZENA. How are you in bed?

DOTTY. Umm…usually on the left.

ZENA. No. What are your techniques like? What tricks do you know?

DOTTY. I can pull a quarter out of my ear.

ZENA. Peaches. Try to concentrate here. I'm talking about sex.

DOTTY. *(terribly embarrassed)* Oh.

ZENA. You've had sex, haven't you?

DOTTY. Ummm, yeah…

ZENA. Do you enjoy it?

DOTTY. Well…My Mama always said, "Good girls don't."

ZENA. I got some very bad news for you, Peaches.

DOTTY. What?

ZENA. Your mama is a moron. Sexual gratification is one of our basic human rights as American citizens. Don't you know that? Don't you get basic cable?

DOTTY. No.

ZENA. Peaches, you got to educate yourself. You got to read the magazines. You can't just leave these things up to nature and expect to keep a man! Now, go home and look at this month's issue –

"The Eighteen Sexual Bliss Secrets," "Forty-two Skills to Satisfy your Man" "Twenty-four Sex Moments that Make Him Scream" I want you to commit them to memory.

DOTTY. Wow. Okay.

ZENA. Okay. You're almost done here. I'm gonna try to hide some of this hair in a flattering sash.

(She ties a flattering sash around **DOTTY***'s head.)*

You know, you don't look too bad. It's surprising, actually.

DOTTY. Yeah? Thanks.

ZENA. I'm even better than I thought. Now get in the back and we'll fit you for some boobs.

DOTTY. Oh my!

ZENA. I think we'll start as big as you can carry and modify as needed. I got some five inch gold pumps you should wear.

DOTTY. Golly! Five inches! How will I walk?

ZENA. You'll take the bus.

DOTTY. Yowza! Ummm…Zena?

ZENA. Yeah?

DOTTY. I really appreciate you doing this for me.

ZENA. Hey, tsall right.

DOTTY. I mean, you're like my best friend in the whole world.

ZENA. Come on, Peaches, you're depressing me now.

DOTTY. No, but I mean, this is really nice, you helping me out. Thanks.

ZENA. Well, you caught me in a good mood here, Peaches.

DOTTY. Yeah?

ZENA. I got my rock last night.

DOTTY. Your rock?

ZENA. Shield your eyes!

(**ZENA** *holds up her hand to show* **DOTTY** *her mammoth diamond ring. It gleams like a laser.*)

I'm engaged!

(**DOTTY** *gasps as if blinded and faints.*)

(*BLACKOUT*)

(*In the darkness there is the sound of cat calls. Men's voices.*)

VOICES. Hey, baby, baby, baby.

(*kissing noises*)

Ohhhhh, hot stuff, give me some of your sweet…

(*wolf whistles*)

Hey mamasita. Can I get some fries with that shake?

(*tongue roll noise – like Tigger rrrrrrrrrrrrrrrrrrrrrrrr*)

Oh, honey, come and get it. Come on, you know you want it.

Oooooo baby baby baby baby baby baby baby…

(*Lights up on* **DOTTY** *running for the bus. She wears a jumpsuit almost identical to her previous one, except that this one has a zebra skin pattern, enormous breasts and ample hips. Her make-up is generous but attractive. Big hair in a flattering sash. She looks, in fact, a lot like* **ZENA**.

She is absolutely terrified at the attention she is getting. Looks around madly before boarding the bus, and rushes for the only empty seat.

Exhausted and panting, she scoots down so as not to be noticed, though it is obvious that even on the bus she is getting leered at. She buries herself in her issue of "Beautiful or Bust.")

(**BARB** [**DAN**] *gets on. She is in a black pants suit. She carries "Hear Me Roar" magazine.*)

DAN. *(Stopping next to* **DOTTY***. Derisively)* Hey. Shove over.

DOTTY. *(startled)* I'm sorry, were you talking to me or…

DAN. Or do you own the world?

DOTTY. Do I…

DAN. A few men drool over you, I guess you own the world.

DOTTY. Oh. No. Or…I'm sorry. I don't think I understand…

DAN. Fine. I'll just stand.

DOTTY. Oh, no! Please! Have a seat! I didn't…Please!

(She slides in with difficulty and **BARB** *sits beside her.* **DOTTY** *smiles at her winningly, and then, getting no response, returns to "Beautiful or Bust.")*

DAN. *(sneering)* You read that trash?

DOTTY. Pardon?

DAN. That fascist, propagandist, woman-hating rag? You subscribe to that?

DOTTY. Oh, no, this is Zena's.

DAN. Zena's.

DOTTY. She's my best friend. She loaned it to me so I could learn how to be a real woman.

DAN. You're joking, right?

DOTTY. Huh?

DAN. That garbage is nothing but male institutional dominance creating a mythology about the feminine image in order to continue their socio-economic stranglehold on our society. It's not about beauty. It's not about sex. It's not about fashion. It's about economics and power.

DOTTY. Mostly I've been looking at the pictures.

DAN. You think there's some universal ideal of beauty captured on those pages? It's all bull shit. Most cultures have vastly opposing sexual ideals. The Maori consider a fat vulva to be of utmost appeal.

DOTTY. Huh.

DAN. The Padung admire droopy breasts.

DOTTY. Really?

DAN. Do you enjoy being objectified?

DOTTY. Ummm...

DAN. Do you crave attention from men on the street who assume that your physical appearance is some sort of invitation to sex?

DOTTY. Gee, I don't know. See, this is only the first time I've ridden the bus.

DAN. When men are drawn to you, not for your thoughts, ideas, character, when they are drawn to you for your...

(*indicating with disgust*)

prosthetics, don't you feel cheapened by that?

DOTTY. Cheapened?

DAN. Don't you realize that that sexualization negates the possibility that you will ever be regarded as an equal, with rights to equal voice, equal power, equal pay?

DOTTY. Huh.

DAN. Do you get paid what a man would get paid for the job you do?

DOTTY. Gee, I never thought about it.

DAN. Maybe you should think about it. What do you do?

DOTTY. I paint toilets on ladies' fingernails.

DAN. (*Pause. Totally mystified and disgusted*) This is all just a big joke to you, isn't it?!

DOTTY. No!

DAN. Look, what's your name?

DOTTY. Umm...Peaches.

DAN. (*disgusted*) Peaches.

DOTTY. Yeah. Well, actually...Dotty. What's yours?

DAN. Barb. Listen, Dotty. There's a meeting you need to go to this week at the Women's Center on Farleigh. Here's a flyer.

DOTTY. Oh, how nice! Thank you!

(*reading*)

"The New Woman for the New Millennium."

DAN. There will be some excellent guest speakers. Myself included. In fact, you're going to be one of my chief topics.

DOTTY. Me? Really? But we just met!

DAN. If only that were true.

DOTTY. *(noticing)* Oh! Darn! It's on Saturday. My husband is usually home on Saturday when he's not with his fiancee, my best friend Zena, and he doesn't allow me to leave the apartment so I don't think I could sneak out. But thanks so much for the invite! Hope you have a nice speech, Barb. Oh gosh! Here's my stop! Gotta run.

DAN. *(shoving "Hear Me Roar" at her)* Look, Dotty. You take this.

DOTTY. "Hear me Roar." Gee. I can barely make it through this magazine. I don't know…

DAN. Take it. I won't be able to sleep tonight if you don't.

DOTTY. Oh. Okay then. Thanks, Barb. Maybe I'll see you again – we could be bus buddies!

DAN. Good God in Heaven.

> *(***DOTTY** *rushes off. Lights fade.*
>
> *In the darkness we hear more catcalls.)*
>
> Oh mama, shake it, don't break it!
> Come take a ride on the loooove train!
> Hubba bubba baby.
>
> *(And more of the same.*
>
> *A clock tower chimes six times.*
>
> *From offstage we hear Dotty.)*

DOTTY. Holy Moly!

> *(Lights come up on ***DOTTY***, rushing to her kitchen table. She grabs chopped meat and a plate and starts making patties.)*

Six o'clock! And I haven't even started Hamel's dinner!

> *(We hear footsteps.)*

I hear footsteps. Do you hear footsteps? It must be Hamel! Heavens! He's coming home and he's early! Heavens!

(**HAMEL** *enters in his service station uniform.*)

HAMEL. *(click click)* Hey kid. Business meal. Change and run.

(*He passes through as if to exit into the bedroom and then suddenly stops, boing!, face out to the audience, digesting what he has just half-seen.*)

HAMEL. Heh?

(*A triple take to* **DOTTY.**)

What the...Woah.

DOTTY. Hamel?

HAMEL. You look...different.

DOTTY. Yes, Hamel Dear?

HAMEL. You look very different.

DOTTY. I do, Hamel?

HAMEL. I can't exactly put my finger on it, but something about you looks very, very different.

DOTTY. Oh! Well...

HAMEL. You been down to the laundry room again?

DOTTY. Yes, Hamel! That's very good Hamel. That was just what I was about to explain. I was down in the laundry room and there was this zebra skin jumpsuit just sitting there and...

HAMEL. *(approaching her)* I like this zebra skin jumpsuit.

DOTTY. And there was this attractive sash for my hair and...

HAMEL. *(coming to her)* I like this attractive sash for your hair.

DOTTY. And there were these enormous...

HAMEL. I like. I like.

(*He scoops her up in his arms and begins to carry her off into the bedroom. He pauses a moment so that she can talk to the audience.*)

DOTTY. Gee! You know, it turns out that my bus buddy Barb was right. I do feel cheap!

(**HAMEL** *sweeps her off to the bedroom as LIGHTS SHIFT.*

The following morning. **DOTTY** *comes out, still dressed as she was, but askew. Her attractive ribbon is untied, her makeup is smudged, and her enormous breasts are vertical rather than horizontal. She is exhausted.*)

DOTTY. *(to us)* Zena's plan to help me win Hamel back was a stroke of genius! He seemed to like me very very much again and didn't even go to his business meal last night.

(coming downstage)

So I know I should feel happy happy happy. Of course I should.

But…it was so strange! There I was, locked in a passionate embrace with my own true love, Hamel, yet all I could hear was the voice of my new bus buddy, Barb.

(We hear the ghostly, reverberating voice of **BARB**.*)*

DAN. When men are drawn to you, not for your thoughts, ideas, character, when they are drawn to you for your… prosthetics, don't you feel cheapened by that?

DOTTY. Yes, Barb. Yes, I do.

DAN. Don't you realize that that sexualization negates the blah blah blah blah blah?

DOTTY. Well, I couldn't remember all that Barb said, but what I could remember struck quite a chord. Do I really want to win Hamel back if everything he loves about me came off a shelf?

(She looks down at her lopsided falsies, struggles to right them, and finally gives up, pulling them out of her jumpsuit through the neck hole. With the falsies out, in her tight jumpsuit, it becomes clear that she has grown quite a belly.)

Goodness! I really must stop eating! Obviously you can't be a real woman and eat too. Oh, what's happening to me? Everything is topsy turvis!

(She picks up "Beautiful or Bust" and "Hear Me Roar" and regards them both.)

Life was so much simpler when I never left the apartment!

(noting the time)

Jeepers! Time to bustle off to work. Maybe I'll see my bus buddy, Barb on the way, and she can help answer some of these troubling questions!

(She puts her falsies and her magazines under her arm and rushes out the door.

DOTTY *enters the bus, looking for her bus buddy,* **BARB**. *She is nowhere to be seen. The only empty seat is next to an enormously pregnant woman [***DAN***], reading "Southern Nursing Mommy" magazine.)*

DAN. *(Seeing her and making room. With a sweet, Southern accent)* Hey, Sweetie! Ya'll come sit right over here!

DOTTY. Oh. Thanks!

(She sits.)

DAN. Isn't it just awful how nobody gives you his seat here? Back in Alabama even a crippled blind man would jump to his feet when he saw a woman in our condition. When ya'll due?

DOTTY. Oh. I paint toilets on ladies' fingernails.

DAN. *(laughing way out of proportion)* No, you silly willy! I said *when*, not *what*! I'm due in three weeks and just as grumpy and tired as a toad in a leap-frog contest. How much weight you put on so far?

DOTTY. Goodness, is it that obvious? Oh dear.

DAN. I've gained forty-two. Bout as comfy as a bison in a bikini. Plum forgot what my feet look like!

DOTTY. *(looking for her)* You're wearing blue shoes with kind of silvery buckle things…

DAN. *(laughing hysterically)* You are too much! What's your name, Sugar?

DOTTY. …Dotty, I guess.

DAN. Right pleased to meet you, Dotty I Guess. I'm Sally Mae.

DOTTY. Hi, Sally Mae. Nice to meet you too.

DAN. Good to have pals in the same boat, right? Hey, maybe down the road a patch we can set up some play dates. Wouldn't that be fun?

DOTTY. *(a bit suspicious of this)* Play dates? Okay...

DAN. You gonna stay home?

DOTTY. I'm supposed to. Hamel thinks I'm there right now. But, I don't know. Now that I'm out I don't think I could just stay home again.

DAN. Well, I'm very disappointed in you, Dotty.

DOTTY. You are?

DAN. I think women who don't stay home and breast feed their babies till they're five years old are going straight to hell, don't you?

(holding up her magazine)

You subscribe?

DOTTY. *(reading)* "Southern Nursing Mommy."

(now very confused)

No. I...I've been trying to read *this*, but I can never seem to find the time.

DAN. "Beautiful or Bust"? Dotty, back where I come from we call that pornography. You shouldn't be reading that, a nice girl like you!

DOTTY. I shouldn't?

(holding up "Hear Me Roar")

Should I be reading this?

DAN. That's even worse! Your husband lets you fill your head with that blasphemy?

DOTTY. He doesn't know about it, actually.

DAN. Well, I'm not surprised. Shame on you, Dotty!

DOTTY. I'm sorry, Sally Mae. I'm just trying to find out how to be a real woman.

DAN. Sugar, bringin babies into this world and raisin 'em up right, that's what it is to be a real woman.

DOTTY. But, Sally Mae, I'm not bringing babies into this world and I'm not...

DAN. Course you are. In bout three months from what I can see.

(*She pats* **DOTTY**'s *belly.*)

I'm guessin it's a girl and I'm never wrong.

DOTTY. Oh! No! Sally Mae, I know how it looks, but I'm just getting plump.

(**SALLY MAE** *guffaws with laughter.*)

DAN. Just gettin plump! That's a good one! Yeah, me too. Just gettin plump!

(**DOTTY** *is thoroughly unnerved by this.*)

(*noticing she's laughing alone*) Well, you are teasin' me, right Sugar? You're joshin', right?

DOTTY. (*staring at her*) I don't...Oh dear! I'm so confused!

DAN. Well, of course you are! Are you worried and clumsy and sick and tired and can't tell which side is up?

DOTTY. Yes!

DAN. That's the miracle of motherhood!

DOTTY. Oh my lord!

DAN. Dotty, Honey, you're pregnant!

DOTTY. Oh my! Holy moly! Good golly! Jeez Louise! Oh my goodness good gracious! Heavens! Lordy day! Good gracious me!

DAN. Well, surely you knew? Didn't you think it odd when your monthly caller stopped payin' his visit?

DOTTY. I tried not to think about it. That's what my Mama always told me, "If something worries you, try not to think about it." Oh, Sally Mae! I can't be pregnant now. My life is at sixes and sevens!

DAN. Sugar, it's time you go pee in a cup.

DOTTY. Will that help?

DAN. And then get yourself to a doctor A.S.A.P. Here.

(*giving her a card*)

Here's my Ob-Gyn. And you take this issue of "Southern Nursing Mommy."

DOTTY. *(wailing)* I have so much to read!!! I feel sick!

DAN. Go eat a cracker, Sweetie.

DOTTY. *(gasping)* Oh, no! Here's my stop!

DAN. Congratulations, Pumpkin!

DOTTY. Bye Sally Mae! Thank you! Maybe I'll see you on the bus again sometime! Bye!

(rushing off)

Lordy day! Pregnant! Heavens!

(ZENA's Beauty Emporium sign drops down.)

(alternately distressed and thrilled) I'm going to have a baby! I'm pregnant! I've got a bun in the oven! I'm a Mommy! Great with child! Knocked up! In the family way!

(Another sign drops down from the ceiling. It reads "Nail-Painting by Peaches" There is the sound of breaking glass.)

Oh dear!

(She rushes into ZENA's Beauty Emporium. There is the sound of things being broken and smashed and a roar from ZENA.)

Zena, are you all right?

(Another roar and the sound of things crashing.)

Zena?

(ZENA comes stumbling out. She is a mess. She looks like she's been crying and drinking. She carries a near-empty pint of whiskey.)

ZENA. Hullo, Peaches.

DOTTY. Zena, I've never seen you like this! Did more British Royalty die?

ZENA. He stood me up.

DOTTY. Who?

ZENA. Derk the jerk. He stood me up last night.

DOTTY. Oh dear.

ZENA. That shithead is two-timing me. I'm gonna cut off his nuts.

DOTTY. Oh dear.

ZENA. And you want to hear the worst part?

DOTTY. Well…

ZENA. You want to hear the worst part?

DOTTY. Ummm…

ZENA. *(getting furious and loud and ugly)* You want to hear the worst part, Peaches??!! You want to hear the worst part??? You want to hear the worst part???

DOTTY. Uh…Yes?

ZENA. I think the asshole is two-timin me with his *wife!*

DOTTY. Oh dear.

ZENA. The indignity! Nobody does that to Zena! I'm gonna kill him. First I'm gonna cut off his nuts, then I'm gonna break up with him, and then I'm gonna kill him.

DOTTY. That sounds awfully drastic.

ZENA. Which part?

DOTTY. You don't know for certain he's cheating. I mean, maybe he was just detained by work.

ZENA. Zena knows. Zena always knows. Now, how should I do it? Knife? Gun? Poison?

DOTTY. Zena, you don't want to kill him. I mean, don't you love him?

ZENA. Of course I love him. If I didn't love him I wouldn't want to kill him.

DOTTY. *(to us)* I have so much to learn.
Zena, won't you miss him if he's gone?

ZENA. Well…yeah. I guess.

DOTTY. Who would you have dinner with?

ZENA. I hadn't thought about it.

DOTTY. You don't want to kill him and then have regrets, do you?

ZENA. *(A sinking moment. Deeply deeply depressed)* Oh Peaches. Why would he cheat on me? *I'm* the one men always two-time *with!*
Look at me, Peaches.

(dragging her close)

I'm getting old, aren't I? Old and ugly. My looks are going.

DOTTY. I think you look swell.

ZENA. Yes, I'm a brilliant cosmetologist. Yes, I'm sophisticated and charming, but really it's been my beauty that got me where I am.

Why didn't I see this coming? Why didn't I develop other strengths? Kindness? Math skills? A sense of humor?

DOTTY. It's not too late! You could learn bridge!

ZENA. *(Looks in the mirror. Smacks herself in the face three times.)* Snap out of it Zena! You still got some gorgeous left in you, baby. It might not be a lot, but it's more than most.

(Takes a swig of whiskey. Rejuvenated:)

Peaches, I'm gonna get Derk back!

DOTTY. Bowling is fun!

ZENA. I'm gonna make him mine again. And then I'm gonna punish him.

DOTTY. How about origami?

ZENA. But how? I've never been in this position. No one's ever cheated on me with his wife before.

DOTTY. Yeah...

ZENA. His wife!

DOTTY. Yeah?

ZENA. That's it! We'll kill his wife! Then all my problems will be solved!

DOTTY. Oh, Zena, you don't even know her. Maybe she's really a lovely person.

ZENA. Nah. I told ya. She's an earthworm. The world will be better off without her.

DOTTY. It will?

ZENA. Now, how should we do this? If I make Derk kill her and then marry me, that's gonna look bad. And if I kill her and then marry Derk, that's gonna look bad too.

DOTTY. It just looks bad, Zena.

ZENA. You're gonna have to do it, Peaches!

DOTTY. Me?

ZENA. You're perfect.

DOTTY. I am?

ZENA. You got a clean record. You got nothing to gain. Who would ever suspect you? And if you disappear, nobody's gonna miss you.

DOTTY. I do have a husband…

ZENA. Yeah, but he's with some other chick, right?

DOTTY. *(miserable)* Yeah…

ZENA. I mean, honestly, what were the chances that you were gonna win him back? It was a long shot, Peaches.

DOTTY. Oh, I don't know…

ZENA. No. It's you, Peaches. It's gotta be you. Now, I'll talk with Derk about it – find out the wife's habits, her daily whereabouts, the best way to off her…

DOTTY. Couldn't the two of you just run away together?

ZENA. I got the Emporium here Peaches! I got people who count on me to fulfill their beauty needs. That's very selfish of you, Peaches. No, you're the one who's expendable in the whole equation.

DOTTY. I have to leave?

ZENA. Well, sure. If you stay around here eventually they'll nab you and prod you and you'll crack like a bad egg about it being Derk and my's idea. No, you gotta leave Sterno.

DOTTY. I feel like I just got here.

ZENA. Yeah. It's too bad really. You were bringing in a nice stream of clientele. And…well…I'll miss you, Peaches.

DOTTY. You will?

ZENA. You're really the first woman friend I've ever had.

DOTTY. You consider me a woman?

ZENA. Well, yeah, Peaches. I mean, what are you, an eggplant?

DOTTY. Oh my gosh. You consider me a real woman! And a friend!

ZENA. You're basically the only woman I could ever tolerate. Probably your obsequious nature.

DOTTY. Gee, thanks Zena! Wow.

ZENA. So, you'll do it? You'll off Derk's wife?

DOTTY. Well…

ZENA. Oh, come on. Be a pal.

DOTTY. Maybe Derk won't want me to off his wife. Maybe he really loves her and will be miserable without her.

ZENA. What a repulsive notion, Peaches. Jeez.

DOTTY. I think you should talk to Derk.

ZENA. Yeah, yeah. But if he gives the thumbs up, you'll do it?

DOTTY. Well… *(forlorn)* If Derk says he wants her gone, if he really doesn't love her, if the possibility of her mothering his children and seeing him into his old age means nothing to him, I guess I'll kill her off.

ZENA. Oh, this is great, Peaches!

(catching sight of herself in the mirror)

Holy shit, I gotta pull myself together. Disgusting, acting this way over a man.

(She takes a last swig and then tosses out the whiskey bottle.)

Awright. I'll go restore perfection. You go put on your boobs – your gut is hangin' out. We got a client coming in fifteen minutes.

(She exits to the back.

DOTTY *begins trying to stuff the falsies down her jumpsuit. Struggles a bit, then quits. Thinks for a long moment.)*

DOTTY. Zena?

ZENA. *(from offstage)* I'm workin' here.

DOTTY. Zena, I need to talk to you.

ZENA. What?

DOTTY. Come out here, please. There's something we need to discuss.

ZENA. *(She comes in, applying an eyelash.)* You're interruptin' my train of thought here, Peaches. What?

DOTTY. What does a man get for offing someone?

ZENA. Huh?

DOTTY. How much does a man make for doing that sort of work?

ZENA. Shit, Peaches. How the fuck would I know?

DOTTY. Well, if I'm going to do this job, I expect to be paid what a man would be paid.

ZENA. Well, smell you.

(Considers her for a moment.)

Huh. Aright, I'll call some friends and find out what the goin' rate is for offing someone.

DOTTY. Thank you.

ZENA. Course I'll expect a discount since we're so close and all, but if Derk does some fishin' in the gas station coffers, and I call in some favors, we can put you on the lam in style.

DOTTY. All right then.

ZENA. Aright.

(She starts to head back again.)

DOTTY. Oh, and Zena?

ZENA. Yeah?

DOTTY. How much do men get paid for painting toilets on finger nails?

ZENA. *(threatening)* Don't push it, Peaches.

(She continues out.)

DOTTY. Ok!

(to us)

Well.

(coming downstage)

I'm a real woman. And pregnant. And an appliance manicurist. And possibly a hit man. That's a lot, when all I ever wanted to be was Hamel's wife.

Owww. My head hurts it's so full. I wish it were the end of the day so I could go home to think.

(The beauty emporium flies off and **DOTTY***'s kitchen table flies in.)*

Yowza!

(The clock tower chimes six times.)

Holy Moly! Six o'clock and I haven't even started Hamel's dinner!

(She begins her hamburger patty rush and then stops.)

I'm gonna put my old clothes back on. I don't want to feel cheap when I tell Hamel about the baby. 'Scuse me.

(She ducks behind the kitchen table and changes into her house dress. Only her head peaks out as she talks.)

I wonder what he'll say. I have absolutely no idea. It used to be I'd always know what Hamel would say. I'd know what I would say and then what Hamel would say and then what I would say back and then what Hamel would say all through each day and into the next.

Now I don't even know what I'm going to say.

(She emerges in her house dress. We hear footsteps. **DOTTY** *opens her mouth and then stops herself.)*

I bet you thought I was going to say, "I hear footsteps." But I'm not. You see what I mean?

HAMEL. *(entering) (click click)* Hey, Kid. I rushed right home to...

(He sees **DOTTY***.)*

DOTTY. Hello, Hamel.

HAMEL. Huh? You look...different. Or, you look the same. Like you used to look.

DOTTY. Yes, Hamel.

HAMEL. Wha happened? Where's the...

DOTTY. Hamel, I need very much to talk to you. About something very important. And I didn't want any distracting apparatus to get in the way of your hearing me.

HAMEL. I thought…I mean, I was expecting you to look like yesterday.

DOTTY. Yes. I know, Hamel.

HAMEL. I came right home specifically anticipating you would look like…Hey, why don't you go down to the laundry room, come back up and we could talk then?

DOTTY. No, Hamel.

HAMEL. No? How come?

DOTTY. I have something very important to tell you.

HAMEL. Yeah…Oh boy. Uhh…I got a business meeting!

(He rushes off to the bedroom.)

*(The following all overlaps – **HAMEL** never hears the news.)*

DOTTY. Wait! Hamel, please. Something thrilling has happened.

HAMEL. Yeah. I'm real late, Kid. I gotta run.

DOTTY. Hamel, you're going to be a…

HAMEL. Hey. Where's my heliotrope shirt?

DOTTY. Hamel, please…

HAMEL. I left a…a client waitin' for a long time. Boy, am I gonna catch it.

DOTTY. Hamel, I'm pregnant! We're going to have a baby! We're going to be a family!

HAMEL. *(rushing out in his heliotrope shirt)* See ya later, Kid.

DOTTY. Hamel…

HAMEL. Don't leave the apartment! Unless you go down to the laundry room. That would be good.

DOTTY. But…

HAMEL. Like my Papa always said, "*Don't leave the apartment.*" Bye, Kid.

DOTTY. Hamel…

(He's gone.)

Hamel…

(pause)

Who *is* Hamel? Who *is* he?

(an idea)

Excuse me.

(She goes to the VCR and plays the tape of her meeting with **HAMEL** *again. We see the meeting, the faint, the whistle, the "What a nut."* **DOTTY** *turns it off.)*

What *was* that? Those people are like strangers. Well, those people actually are strangers, but...what was I thinking? I played that over and over again. In my head, too. What was I thinking?

I got to start paying better attention. I'm gonna be somebody's mom soon. Somebody's gonna look up to me. Look to me for what's right. For how to be. And I don't have a clue.

I better get a clue.

(BLACKOUT)

*(***ZENA***'s Beauty Emporium.* **ZENA** *is taking down the "Nail Painting by Peaches" sign. She is very excited.*

DOTTY *enters quietly in her house dress.)*

ZENA. *(rapid fire)* Ah! Peaches! Great! It's all set! Last night Derk and I rendezvoused and we're on. He borrowed some bucks from the gas station and you'll be sittin pretty wherever you wind up, believe you me. But we gotta hurry.

(She grabs a pile of black clothes.)

Here, put these on. Just put em over what you're wearing, they're huge. Come on, get the lead out! We gotta do it now before he gets cold feet.

DOTTY. *(very muffled)* He wants to off her?

ZENA. No, he wants to throw her a surprise party. Of course he wants to off her! Here.

(She takes the large black sweatshirt and puts it over **DOTTY**'s *head.)*

Putcher arms through. Great! That looks great. Here, put your foot in here.

*(She takes the enormous black sweat pants and holds out
a leg to* DOTTY. DOTTY *complies.)*

Jeez, Peaches. You're a little slow today, even for you.
You want a latte?

DOTTY. He wants to kill his wife? You're sure?

ZENA. He got me the money didn't he? And the gun. This
is very serious business. The whole enterprise is puttin
Derk and me at mucho mucho risk, Peaches. You
better not botch this thing up. Now you only handle
the gun with gloves on, capiche? Here, put em on.

DOTTY. So, he doesn't love her. He says he doesn't love her.

ZENA. Hello? Earth to Peaches.

DOTTY. Did he say that? Did he say he didn't love her?

ZENA. Well, maybe I'm being too interpretational or something, but I think it's kinda implied by the fact that HE
WANTS HER DEAD! Now put on the friggin' gloves
here, Peaches. You're makin me a nervous friggin'
wreck!

DOTTY. You're right. He doesn't love her. He wants her
dead.

ZENA. Hey, you sick or somethin? You look weird.

DOTTY. No, I'm fine. I'm gonna be fine. Give me those
gloves. I'll do it.

ZENA. Good for you. Now, it's all written out here, you gotta
memorize it and destroy the paper.

DOTTY. Where's the money?

ZENA. Nu uh. You get the money *after* you do the job.

DOTTY. I won't be coming back here after I do the job. I
want the money now.

ZENA. What do you think, I'm nuts? I give you the money
now, you run off, don't kill the wife, then what?

DOTTY. I'll kill her. Don't worry.

ZENA. No friggin' way.

DOTTY. Then forget it.

ZENA. *(stares at her a moment)* What happened to you? You're
scarin' me, Peaches.

(no answer)

Aright aright. You've put me in an uncompromiseable situation, Peaches. Here's the money.

(She hands her a sack. **DOTTY** *looks in. It's a lot of money.)*

DOTTY. *(to herself)* Holy Moly.

(To **ZENA**, *very cool)*

This will work.

ZENA. Damn straight it'll work. Now here's the gun. When you want to fire it, you cock this and pull the trigger. You think you can remember that?

DOTTY. I want the manicure set too.

ZENA. What, are you gonna file her to death?

DOTTY. I want the manicure set.

ZENA. You're gonna keep doin the toilet nails?

DOTTY. Maybe.

ZENA. I'm not sure I like the idea of you paintin' my toilet for someone else.

DOTTY. It's not really up to you. You have no more say about anything I do. You get Derk. I get me.

ZENA. Shit Peaches. You're bein' so weird. It's like I don't even know you.

DOTTY. I know. Me too. Where's the manicure set?

(It appears.)

ZENA. Here. Listen, could you at least not use the name Peaches any more? If I get a new assistant I'll name her Peaches and keep the sign.

DOTTY. All right. I'm not Peaches any more anyway.
Well, I guess I'm off.

ZENA. Oh, wait. Here.

(She puts a black ski mask over **DOTTY**'s *head.)*

DOTTY. *(a moment)* Bye Zena.

ZENA. Yeah, yeah.

DOTTY. Good luck with Derk. I hope he doesn't hire someone to off *you* down the line.

ZENA. Jesus.

(**DOTTY** *starts out.* **HAMEL** *rushes in, stopping her.*)

HAMEL. Oh, thank God. Thank God you're still here! Peaches, right?

ZENA. Derk, what are you doin here?! Get back to the station – we gotta get our alibis straight like we talked about. Jeez. Go Peaches! Go!

HAMEL. No. Wait. Don't go Peaches. I want out. I don't want to do this, Zena.

ZENA. What??? What are you talkin about?

HAMEL. I can't kill her. It was crazy. I got all confused in the head. I was talkin crazy last night. Peaches, give me back the gun.

ZENA. Hold on a minute. What about me? What about us gettin married? You made a commitment here.

HAMEL. I'm sorry. I just can't go through with this. I…I love her.

ZENA. You what?

DOTTY. You what?

HAMEL. I love her. I love my wife. I come home and there she is. That's good. I don't want to come home and she's not there. That would be bad. I don't want to kill her. Peaches, give me back the gun. Give me back the money. It's over.

(*There is a long pause while* **DOTTY** *considers this.*)

DOTTY. No.

HAMEL. Huh?

DOTTY. No. It's too late.

HAMEL. Huh?

DOTTY. Your wife is already dead.

HAMEL. I'm too late?

DOTTY. You're too late.

HAMEL. Oh God. Oh my God.

(*He staggers.*)

(**ZENA** *goes to him and slaps him, hard.*)

ZENA. Jerk!

HAMEL. Oh God.

(She slaps him again.)

HAMEL. Oh God.

(She slaps him again, three times. He grabs her, kisses her passionately and they fall into their usual embrace.

DOTTY *quietly takes the bag and the manicure set and leaves.*

The bus. **DOTTY** *gets on in her full black attire, mask and all, and sits down next to* **DAN.** *He is a nervous, depressed, poindexter with thick glasses, centrally parted hair and a bow tie. He has a very large briefcase. He is reading a magazine and looks up worriedly as* **DOTTY** *slides in beside him.)*

DAN. Oh dear.

(A pause as he regards her.)

Have you just been to a…funeral?

DOTTY. I'm offing someone.

DAN. Oh.

DOTTY. It pays very well. I'm about to be a single mother, so that's an important consideration.

(pause)

What are you reading?

DAN. "Field and Stream and Guns and Ammo and Sports and Weightlifting Magazine." My wife thinks I'm not a real man. She's hoping this will help.

DOTTY. Is it helping so far?

DAN. I don't think so.

(a moment)

Isn't that mask hot?

DOTTY. It's not very comfortable. But it sure beats a facial. You ever get one of those?

DAN. No. I'm a man!

DOTTY. Hey, how come you're not at work? Aren't all the men at work now?

DAN. I'm a door-to-door salesman. I'm traveling to the next densely-populated area to peddle my wares.

DOTTY. What do you sell?

DAN. Single volume encyclopedias and maps.

DOTTY. Those are just the kinds of things a person on the lam would need!

DAN. The encyclopedias are outdated and you can get a map at any gas station for much less.

DOTTY. Great! I'll take them!

(Reaching in the bag and pulling out a handful of money.)

DAN. The facts are iffy and the destinations are terrible.

DOTTY. They'll be fine. Please.

DAN. Well…All right.

(He reaches into his briefcase and gets an encyclopedia.)

What maps would you like?

DOTTY. It doesn't matter, really. I haven't been anywhere but Sterno, so anywhere else will be different.

DAN. *(handing her a pile)* Here you go.

DOTTY. This is so amazing. Everything I need I seem to find on the bus. Oh! Next stop is mine!

DAN. Wait! Do you ride here often? Maybe we could be bus buddies! What's your name?

DOTTY. Sorry. I don't have a name any more. And today's my last day on this bus line. But it was swell meeting you! You seem like a real man to me. Gotta run. Bye!

(She hops off the bus.)

DAN. I seem like a real man.

(He considers this a moment, then, with a surprised smile, throws the magazine out the window.)

(BLACKOUT)

*(**DOTTY**'s kitchen table. **DOTTY** enters. She pulls off her ski mask and regards what used to be her whole world.)*

DOTTY. I better get this over with.

(Looks around, thinking.)

Guess the bedroom's the best place. Not that Dotty would have been in the bedroom at this time of day. Dotty never had anywhere to go, but she was an early riser and greeted each day with spirit and gusto. She would have been merrily at work on one of her many art projects, here at the kitchen table.

But it's just too messy to do it out here. Too sad. No, the bedroom is better. Excuse me.

(She pulls on the ski mask and pulls out the gun. Cocks it.

Exits into the bedroom.

There is a long silence. Then a gunshot. Another long silence. The sound of weeping. **DOTTY** *comes out, pulls off the ski mask. Cries softly to herself for a moment.)*

I did it. She's gone. Dotty's gone.

She was so sweet, really. So hopeful. I'll miss her, I really will.

Excuse me. I think I need a bit of a cry.

(She has a bit of a cry. Pulls herself together.)

All right. That's enough. No more harping on the past.

(Mops up her tears with the mask.)

Time to get on with my life!

(looking around)

I wonder what I should take?

(She regards the falsies, decides no; examines her stack of magazines, decides no; picks up her toilet sculpture, decides no.

She puts the encyclopedia and maps in the bag with her money.)

That's a start, anyway.

(to the audience)

I know one of you has my picture of Hamel. It's okay, you can keep it. Just cross out "Hamel" and write "Derk" on the back. It's still a nice picture.

Well, I guess this is goodbye then. I won't be taking you with me. Sorry. I sort of need to make a fresh start, cut down on distractions, learn how to focus. Soon there'll be someone who's going to need all my attention. Like my Mama always said...

(pause)

But...I'm the mama now.

(Regards her belly. Takes a moment to think.)

Time for us to start.

(Picks up her bag and her manicure kit.)

First step, first. Choose a new bus line. Out of Sterno.

(Takes out a map.)

I wonder who we'll meet.

(She starts out. Over her shoulder.)

Turn out the lights on your way out.

(LIGHTS FADE)

End of Play

Also by
Deborah Zoe Laufer...

End Days

The Last Schwartz

Please visit our website **samuelfrench.com** for complete
descriptions and licensing information

Printed in the United States
139166LV00001B/10/P